Rachel Isadora

Caribbean Dream

G. P. Putnam's Sons

New York

To my father

Excerpt from The Child's Return *reproduced with permission of Curtis Brown Ltd, London, on behalf of the Estate of Phyllis Shand Allfrey. Copyright Phyllis Shand Allfrey.*

G. P. Putnam's Sons, Reg. U.S. Pat. & Tm. Off. Published simultaneously in Canada.
Printed in Hong Kong. Book designed by Donna Mark. Text set in Calisto.
The art was done in watercolor on Strathmore 500 Bristol.
Library of Congress Cataloging-in-Publication Data
Isadora, Rachel. Caribbean dream / Rachel Isadora. p. cm.
Summary: A lyrical and evocative dreamscape of the Caribbean.
[1. Caribbean area—Fiction. 2. Dreams—Fiction.] I. Title.
PZ7.1763Car 1998 [E]—dc21 97-49630 CIP AC
ISBN 0-399-23230-3
1 3 5 7 9 10 8 6 4 2
FIRST IMPRESSION

I remember a far tall island

floating in cobalt paint

The thought of it is a

childhood dream

—*Phyllis Shand Allfrey*
THE CHILD'S RETURN

Where morning
meets light,
we rise.

Where friends

meet friends,

we smile.

Where sound

meets color,

we hide.

Where waves

meet sand,

we swim.

Where sun

meets water,

we fish.

Where sea

meets sky,

we sail.

Where wind

meets hill,

we run.

Where rain

meets earth,

we splash.

Where music
meets hearts,
we sing.

Where song

meets soul,

we dance.

Where years

meet story,

we see.

Where moonlight
meets path,
we walk.

Where darkness
meets light,
       we dream.

We dream.